Thanksgiving

by Meredith Dash

capstone

ABDO
NATIONAL HOLIDAYS
Kids

Photo Credits: AP Images, Glow Images, iStock, Minden Pictures, Thinkstock

Production Contributors: Teddy Borth, Jennie Forsberg, Grace Hansen

Design Contributors: Candice Keimig, Laura Rask, Dorothy Toth

Library of Congress Cataloging-in-Publication data is available on the Library of Congress Website.

ISBN 978-1-4966-0988-5 (paperback)

Table of Contents

Thanksgiving 4
History. 8
Today's Thanksgiving 20
More Facts 22
Glossary 23
Index 24

Thanksgiving

Thanksgiving is about giving thanks. Family and friends **gather** on this day.

Thanksgiving is every November. It is on the fourth Thursday.

GIVE THANKS

History

The **pilgrims** were the first to celebrate Thanksgiving.

The **pilgrims** came to North America by ship. The ship was called the **Mayflower**.

The first winter was hard. Many **pilgrims** did not survive. Then they met the **Native Americans**.

The **Native Americans** could farm, hunt, and fish. They taught the **pilgrims** to do the same.

The **pilgrims** were thankful for the good **harvest**. They invited their **Native American** friends to a **feast**.

The **pilgrims** and **Native Americans** played games. They told stories. They celebrated for three days.

Today's Thanksgiving

Today, many Americans celebrate Thanksgiving. They share a special meal.

More Facts

- Deer, corn, shellfish, meat, and cranberries were eaten at the first Thanksgiving.
- The **pilgrims** were English Protestants. They came to America to break away from the Church of England.
- There were 102 passengers and around 30 crew and sailors on the **Mayflower**. It took them 66 days to cross the Atlantic Ocean.

Glossary

feast – a large meal.

gather – come together.

harvest – what is gathered from ripe crops. A harvest may be vegetables, fruits, or grains.

Mayflower – the ship the Pilgrims sailed from Southampton to the New World.

Native Americans – the very first people who lived in America.

pilgrims – the people who sailed from England in 1620 and settled in Plymouth Rock, Massachusetts.

Index

celebrate 8, 18, 20

family 4

feast 16

friends 4

harvest 16

Mayflower 10

Native Americans 12, 14, 16, 18

North America 10

November 6

pilgrims 8, 10, 12, 14, 16, 18